— Miss Bridie —
Chose a Shovel

by **Leslie Connor**
Illustrated by **Mary Azarian**

HOUGHTON MIFFLIN COMPANY
BOSTON 2004

For Jonathan,
and also for Sam, Marley, and Ian
—L.C.

For Bob Kosturko,
in gratitude for superb book design, creative support,
and friendship
—M.A.

www.houghtonmifflinbooks.com

The text of this book is set in Italian Oldstyle.
The illustrations are woodcuts.

Library of Congress Cataloging-in-Publication Data
Connor, Leslie.
Miss Bridie chose a shovel / by Leslie Connor ;
illustrated by Mary Azarian.
p. cm.
Summary: Miss Bridie emigrates to America in 1856 and chooses to bring a
shovel, which proves to be a useful tool throughout her life.
ISBN 0-618-30564-5
[1. Shovels—Fiction.] I. Azarian, Mary, ill. II. Title.
PZ7.C7644Mi 2004
[E]—dc22
2003012290

Manufactured in the United States of America
WOZ 10 9 8 7 6 5 4 3 2 1

She could have picked a chiming clock or a porcelain figurine, but Miss Bridie chose a shovel back in 1856.

Miss Bridie chose the shovel from the peg in the barn, and she took it to the dock, where she stepped aboard the ship. She leaned on the shovel as she rocked in the cabin while she lived on the ship on her way across the sea.

Miss Bridie flung the shovel with her pack on her shoulder when she stepped off the ship in the harbor in New York.

She brought along the shovel when she rented the room
above the little shop, where she also got a job.

Miss Bridie took her shovel when she got up early, and she
dug a little garden out back behind the shop.

She put her plants in crates when the spring rains came, and she sold them to the ladies for their gardens in New York.

Miss Bridie brought her shovel to the city park in winter, and she cleared a narrow path through the silent falling snow.

She took her shovel down to the frozen, moonlit river, where she scraped away the snow and went skating up and down.

Miss Bridie packed her shovel when she moved to the house
when she married the young man she'd met skating on the river.

She dug all the holes for the posts with her shovel when they
put up the pen for the new goats and sheep.

Miss Bridie planted seeds, which in time became an orchard and a field full of corn on the farm on the hill. She swung the shovel high when she cut into the hill to build the root cellar for the apples from their farm.

Miss Bridie grabbed her shovel when the rains swelled the creek, and she scooped away the mud from the old kitchen step. She carved a bigger pond and she banked it with her shovel so the creek wouldn't come up to the kitchen anymore. Miss Bridie sent the shovel to pry the doctor's buggy from the mud by the pond when her babies were born.

She shoveled lumps of coal into the black iron stove that warmed the little children and browned the loaves of bread.

Miss Bridie hilled the soil in the dry heat of summer, and she worried for the crops as the creek ran dry. She listened to the promise of the

distant rolling thunder, and she waited for the cloudburst to reach their thirsty field. Miss Bridie saw the lightning strike...

...that set their barn on fire, and she raced to free the livestock as the timbers burned away.

Miss Bridie watched the rain as it swept away their fields,
and she wondered if the farm could ever thrive again.
She searched through the ash when the rains quelled the fire,
and she found her shovel blade with the handle burnt away.

Miss Bridie chose a limb from a tree in the orchard, and she worked an apple handle for the old shovel blade.

Once more she turned the soil, and she started raising flowers
on the farm with the children, who grew tall by her side.
She sold her fruit and flowers at a stand by the road, where
the people and the summers just kept passing by.

Miss Bridie sadly trudged up the hill with her shovel when her husband, whom she loved, got sick and passed away.

She planted him a tree and some flowers underneath that
come up like a memory with the warmth of every spring.

Miss Bridie cleared the snow from the frozen pond in winter, and she led her children's children as they skated round and round.

At night she hung her shovel on the peg in the barn, and she stood looking out at the quiet, frosted farm.

She could have had a chiming clock or a porcelain figurine, but Miss Bridie chose a shovel back in 1856.